THE NILE ADVENTURES

THE HEART SCARAB

SAVIOUR PIROTTA

ILLUSTRATED BY
JO LINDLEY

Other books by Saviour Pirotta

Set in the Stone Age:

THE WOLFSONG SERIES

The Stolen Spear

The Whispering Stones

The Mysterious Island

The Wolf's Song

Set in Ancient Greece:

ANCIENT GREEK MYSTERIES

Mark of the Cyclops

Secret of the Oracle

Pirates of the Poseidon

Shadow of the Centaurs

Set in the Islamic Golden Age:

The Golden Horseman of Baghdad

CONTENTS

Poem from an inscription on the underside of a heart scarab

Oh my heart!
Oh my heart, inherited from my mother.
My heart of my different ages.
Do not stand as witness against me.
Do not oppose me in the tribunal.
Do not show hostility against me before the
Keeper of the Balance.
For you are my ka which is in my body.
You are the protector who causes
my limbs to be healthy.
Go forth to the good place to which
we all hasten.
What is good for us is good for the judge.
Let the heart rejoice at the verdict.
Do not speak lies in the presence of the gods.
Behold!
You are distinguished, a justified one.

PART 1

1269 BCE
the tenth year in the reign of Ramesses II

The old man stepped out from under the umbrella on his wicker chariot, leaning heavily on his gold-encrusted walking stick. The afternoon heat was intense and he waited, perspiring and scowling, until the chariot driver removed the umbrella and held it above his head.

A second slave, his head housekeeper, bustled out of the gate in a white shenti embroidered with gold thread.

"Welcome home, master," he said, taking the old man's walking stick and helping him up the marble steps. He signalled to the chariot-driver who returned to the chariot with his umbrella.

The old man's house was practically a palace, one of the finest in all the Black Land. Built on two floors, it was surrounded by a shady orchard of palm trees and flowering bushes. To one side was a large stable full of magnificent horses. Not that the old man ever went there to admire them. He found it impossible to control them. A mare had kicked him when he was still a child and he had walked with a limp ever since. Seventy-eight years of constant pain! No, the old man had slaves to look after the animals and a chariot driver to take him wherever he wanted to go. The horses were only there to impress visitors, to show everyone how wealthy he was.

On the opposite side of the garden lay a swimming pool, glittering a bright blue in the afternoon sun. The old man scowled at the few leaves floating on the water. "Has Talgu not cleaned the pool yet?"

"I ordered her to get out of the sun, master. This heat is not good for her at her age," replied the housekeeper. "She will clean the pool later. Was Master thinking of bathing?"

The old man used the pool often because the warm water soothed the pain in his crippled leg. But now was not the time to bask in perfumed water. Not while there were urgent matters to see to.

"Is the boy here?" he asked the housekeeper as he stepped indoors.

The housekeeper nodded. "They brought him in this morning. I put him in the study chamber as you asked, master," he said as he removed his master's extravagant wig and wiped down his bald head with a scented piece of cloth.

He placed a fresh wig on the old man's head. It was a house wig, simpler than the outdoors one but still made from expensive human hair.

He held up a mirror and the old man turned his head this way and that to make sure the wig was on straight. "Very good, Hotep," he said. "Fetch some beer. And make sure no one disturbs me."

The old man limped past a row of brightly

decorated columns and stopped near a collection of palm trees growing in large gleaming pots. Slipping behind them, he opened a door painted to blend in with the wall around it. This led into a dark corridor and, at the end of it, a second door. The old man unlocked it with a wooden key.

"Good afternoon."

A boy was sat on the polished floor, his hands and feet bound tightly. He looked up and hissed like a cornered snake. He couldn't have been more than twelve or thirteen, the nobleman reckoned, yet he was already starting to stoop. His brown skin was scarred in many places. His dark hair fell in unruly curls around his shoulders. He looked decidedly out of place in the old man's secret chamber; a spacious room with narrow windows set close to the ceiling. A statue of Heka—the ancient god of magic—stood by the door, a knife in one hand and a staff entwined with snakes in the other. There were low tables all around, most of them piled high with papyrus scrolls or wax tablets. One was covered in glass bottles, all filled with brightly coloured liquids. The air was heavy with the smell of incense.

"Who are you?" demanded the boy. "Why have you brought me here?"

"I am but a humble servant of Heka," replied the old man. "A magician! You might call me a hekau."

"Set me free at once," growled the boy, obviously unimpressed by the fine surroundings. "I have done nothing wrong. You might be wealthy but that doesn't give you the right to keep me against my own will."

"My slave will untie your hands and feet in a moment," sneered the nobleman. "You are called Abanoub, are you not?"

"How do you know my name?" snapped the boy, taken aback.

"Abanoub means 'the king of gold'," continued the old man without answering the boy's question. "And yet you can't afford gold thread for your loincloth, your sethi. You are dirt poor. The *unfortunate offspring of paupers."*

"My parents enjoy the delights of the afterlife, sir," said Abanoub defiantly. "They were good people who lived their lives according to the wishes of the gods."

"No doubt," said the old man. "And yet Anubis paid them back by taking them early, leaving you to fend for your brothers and sisters. Does that not make you angry?"

"You are mistaken," replied Abanoub. "I have no family left to look after."

"Poor child," tutted the old man. "Abandoned by gods and *man. I'm sure that must make you absolutely furious."*

Abanoub shrugged. "It is the way things are. I am luckier than most. I have a good job hauling mud bricks on building sites. It earns me enough grain to eat and to barter for anything else I might need."

The old man knew all this already. His trusted slaves had been observing Abanoub for a while.

They had reported every detail of his life to their master, including his lack of family. Indeed, it was this last little detail that had the old man single out Abanoub for his daring plan.

"Your slave approached me while I was having my daily bath in the river," continued Abanoub. "He said he had a job for me, against payment of a gosling. But, when we were alone in the fields, your men attacked me, blindfolded me, tied me up and dragged me here against my will. A fine way to treat an honest bricklayer."

"I apologise on my slaves' behalf," said the old man.

There was a polite knock at the door and Hotep brought in a jug of beer and a golden cup on a tray. He set them down on a table.

"Cut the boy loose," ordered the old man. "And fetch another cup. Our guest must be thirsty."

"Master." Hotep carried out the order without once looking at Abanoub.

"My slave was right when he said there was a

job for you," said the old man, "but it is not the mundane task you might have imagined."

Another knock at the door interrupted him and Hotep returned with a second cup, this one made of simple clay. The old man filled it himself but waited for Hotep to close the door before speaking again.

"Come, you are on the brink of becoming someone powerful, someone to be feared. Let us drink to the gods."

He carried a lamp over to the statue of Heka and lit a fire in a bowl. Bowing his head and muttering an incantation, he did the same with the statue of Thoth. Smoke rose quickly from both bowls, filling the room and stinging Abanoub's eyes.

"Drink!" the old man ordered Abanoub. He watched the boy reluctantly drink but put his own cup down without touching it to his lips. Almost immediately, Abanoub's eyes grew glassy and he started to sway.

"Sir…" he said.

The old man opened a wooden box and took out a golden amulet shaped like two snakes with entwined tails. Their gemstone eyes flashed black and green, the colours of death and destruction, as he held it up. When he hung it round Abanoub's neck, there was a faint smell of singed skin and the boy shuddered but he made no attempt to remove it. He merely stared ahead.

The snakes around his neck looked like they were gobbling each other up.

"Drink again and repeat after me," said the old man. "To Heka. May his ancient magic fill our life in the Black Land and help us at the hour of our parting."

"To Heka, may he fill…" Abanoub tried to say, but his words were slurred.

"Look me in the eyes," said the old man, leaning so close to Abanoub he could see himself reflected in the boy's dark pupils. "Hear my words and obey…"

Abanoub's lips moved but no sound came out.

"Perfect," sniggered the old man, his voice the purr of a dangerous tiger. "Now listen to your master. There is important work to be done..."

The General's Tomb

- Renni -

"Time to go home, everyone." The work manager stuck his head round the doorway of Pharaoh's new tomb. "See you all tomorrow at sunrise."

Renni put down his brush. He'd been painting hieroglyphs since the crack of dawn and his right arm ached with tiredness.

"Your hieroglyphs are improving by the day," said Renni's Uncle Pepy, handing him a brush to clean. "Well done. Make sure you put the paints away properly and don't be up late tonight. I need you to have a clear head tomorrow. We're starting to paint the Book of the Gates."

Renni was an apprentice artist, a *sesh qedut*.

His father had been a gilder, someone who covered statues and sarcophagi with gold leaf. Renni had been hoping to follow in his footsteps but his father had died suddenly, leaving him without a mentor. Luckily, Renni's Uncle Pepy had taken him under his wing. He came from a long line of painters who specialised in decorating tombs and temples. He was training Renni to draw, insisting he use red chalk that he would then correct in black.

"Yes, Uncle, sir," said Renni humbly. "Thank you for the opportunity to let me show what I can do. I am learning fast under your guidance, Uncle, sir."

Uncle Pepy strode away down the corridor while Renni started washing and drying the brushes, making sure that every strand of fibre in them was perfectly clean before wrapping them in linen. He tied the lids down on the paint pots and stowed them away in a large wicker basket. By the time he'd finished, the corridor was mostly empty.

"We're all going to Ipy's for supper," said one of the other apprentices, still packing his master's tools. "He's made some fresh beer with leftover bread. Do you want to come?"

Renni shook his head. "Thanks, but I need to go home early and practise drawing ducks. I'm hoping Uncle Pepy will let me paint some tomorrow."

The other apprentice shrugged. "See you in the morning then."

Finding himself alone, Renni looked up at the large picture his uncle was painting. It showed Ramesses the Great

charging across the desert in his war chariot, wearing the double crown of Kemet, the Black Land. All around him lay the chaos of battle, one in which the Egyptian army had been victorious. The ground was littered with the corpses of slain enemy soldiers. Beady eyed vultures circled the air hungrily.

Even in the fading light, the colours in the picture glowed like polished gemstones. The jet-black in the pharaoh's eye. The royal blue and gold in his crown, meant to show strength and power! The red in the blood, dripping from the beaks of the hungry vultures,

that showed anger but also victory. And the vibrant green in the palm trees all around, which were drawn to look like the wind was actually rippling through their spiky branches.

Renni touched the amulet shaped like the eye of Horus which dangled from his plaited sidelock. It was his most treasured possession, handed down from father to son through the generations. His mother had given it to him on the day he left home to start living in the village of the artists near the Valley of the Kings. "It will protect you and bring you good luck," she'd said.

Renni hoped the amulet would protect him tonight, for he'd lied to his friend. The real reason that he couldn't go to Ipy's for supper wasn't that he wanted to practise drawing ducks. It was because his elder brother Mahu had told him to wait in the tomb, unnoticed.

Mahu had a plan, and his plans usually spelled trouble. Renni hoped he was worrying for nothing. Perhaps Mahu just wanted to have a look around the Valley of the Kings, which was prohibited to people who weren't priests or artists working in the tombs.

Looking for a place to hide, Renni dragged his wicker basket behind an enormous clay jar. It was full of oily water and stank like dead fish, but it was the only hiding place he could find in the rock-cut corridor.

Renni waited. It got dark and a chill spread across the tomb. Renni could hear all kinds of horrible noises he'd not been aware of when it was still light. Things seemed to be slithering across the rocky floor. Other things outside the tomb squeaked and hissed.

Renni's skin started to crawl. Had Meretseger, the snake goddess, discovered him? Had she sent her snakes to punish him for staying in the valley at night? He was about to muster the courage to crawl out of his hiding place and run away when he heard footsteps approaching the tomb. Two sets of them, marching together. Renni shrank back into his hiding place. His heart was beating so loudly, he was sure whoever was coming would hear it.

The footsteps stopped at the doorway.

"All clear in here," said a man's gruff voice. He was obviously a *medjay*, a policeman, making sure that all the workers had left the Valley of the Kings.

"These open tombs give me the creeps," said a second voice. "Wouldn't step in one of them at night if you tripled my wages."

"The whole valley spooks me," agreed the first voice. "Can't wait for my transfer to the Kush to come through."

Renni breathed a sigh of relief as the *medjay* moved on. The moon came up and silvery light reached into the tomb.

Suddenly there was a low cough at the doorway, making him jump.

"Renni, you in there?"

Renni peeped out from behind the clay jar.

A boy was standing in the doorway, his wide shoulders framed by the moonlight. He had a cotton bag slung over his right shoulder.

"Is that you, Mahu?" Renni asked.

"Yes. Come on out. The coast is clear."

"I thought you'd never come." Renni scrambled to his feet, brushing the dust from his loincloth. Mahu was his elder brother but the two of them couldn't look more different. Where Renni was short and baby-faced, still sporting a side-lock, Mahu was tall with a jutting chin and powerful arms.

"Hurry up," ordered Mahu, turning around and walking away from the tomb, "we haven't got all night."

"Where are we going?" Renni

asked as he followed his brother across a dusty path where an ancient tomb was being redecorated for Ramesses's children. It was said the gods had blessed him with many of them.

"Stop asking questions," answered Mahu. "You'll soon find out."

"I was hoping you just wanted to explore a little," said Renni.

"I have more important things to do than play scouting games," snorted Mahu. "Now get a move on."

"I hope we're not going to break the law," said Renni. "Actually, we are already doing that just by being here."

"The law is only there for the powerful and the stupid," snapped his brother. "I'm neither. Now stop whining like a baby."

He led the way round a hill where the valley grew wider, showing tombs on either side. It was eerily quiet except for the shrieking of bats overhead. They made Renni's skin crawl. "Hey," he said suddenly. "I just saw something move."

His brother looked back. "Where?"

Renni pointed to a statue of a cat-headed goddess outside a tomb. "Over there."

Mahu peered around. "I don't see anything."

"I'm sure I saw something move," insisted Renni. "Let's go home."

"Don't be silly, little brother," said Mahu. "It's probably a cat, or a desert fox. Nothing to be scared of."

"Or someone might be following us," said Renni. "It could be the *medjay*."

Mahu looked around one more time, then shrugged and started walking again. "You're imagining things. Come on."

Renni hurried to catch up with him, touching his sidelock amulet for comfort. They passed a grand tomb with statues of the god Amun-Ra on either side of the door and slipped into a narrow pathway behind it. It led to a smaller tomb with a narrow doorway where Mahu stopped.

"This is the grave of a general in the pharaoh's army," he said. "He was filthy rich so there should be plenty of things inside. I've managed to locate a secret tunnel that goes straight to its burial chamber."

Renni's eyes grew wide with terror. "We're breaking into a tomb?"

"*I'm* not," chuckled Mahu. "I'm just standing outside, making sure my little brother doesn't get caught."

Renni stepped away from his brother. "I'm not doing this."

"But you are," said Mahu.

"We'll make the gods angry," argued Renni. "They'll punish us and when we die our hearts will be devoured by the goddess Ammut."

"Do you honestly think that the gods have time to waste on insignificant little boys like you?" said Mahu. "Now shut up and do as I say." He brushed a clump of stinging nettles aside to reveal a small square hole.

"Is that the entrance to the secret tunnel?" asked Renni.

"Yes, aren't I clever to have found it? Mind you, it took me ages to remove the stone."

"Why would a tomb have a secret tunnel?" Renni wanted to know.

"Dishonest builders sometimes work with tomb raiders," replied Mahu. "They leave ways for thieves to get in, and then share the booty. The world is not the honest place you imagine it to be, little brother. Now get in there and come out with something precious. Something we can barter."

Renni crossed his arms across his chest. "I refuse."

"Since Father died, I am your legal guardian," said Mahu. "I can order you to do anything I like and I'm telling you to get in that tomb."

Renni stood his ground. "*You* go if you want some treasure that badly."

"I… can't," said Mahu.

Renni sneered. "Why not?"

"Because I can't."

"You're scared, aren't you?" said Renni. "Admit it. You *are* scared the gods might punish you so you want me to steal instead. You're a coward."

Mahu grabbed his brother by the sidelock. "Stop babbling. Get in there and find something I can barter with, do you hear? Our house is falling to bits. The landlord wants to evict us because we're not looking after it as we should. Mother has hardly anything to eat. You can see her bones poking out at the elbows. So you stand there and tell me your own mother is not worth stealing one piece of jewellery from a wealthy man who is *dead*."

"I still refuse," said Renni although not as assured as a moment earlier. Mahu did have a way of convincing people with his arguing. "Please, let go of my sidelock."

"I'd go in myself," hissed Mahu, not letting go of Renni's hair, "but if something does happen to me there will be no one to look after Mother."

"There'd be me," said Renni.

"Fat lot of good you'd be with your stupid paintbrushes," spat Mahu.

"At least I earn a proper wage," said Renni.

"If you don't go in," snapped Mahu, "I'll sell you into slavery. I have the right. I'd barter you for a fat ram. That will solve our family problems. You'll end up working in some mine for the Kush. Now get in there and watch out for booby traps. These tunnels tend to be riddled with them."

He picked Renni up and shoved him headfirst into the tunnel. "I'm serious, little brother. You come back with at least one piece of treasure or I swear I'll put the stone back in place and leave you to die."

Terrified his brother might actually carry out his threat, Renni wriggled forward on his elbows. He prayed the gods would understand he wasn't breaking into a tomb because he chose to. He was being *forced* to. And perhaps Mahu was just a little bit right. A dead general probably wouldn't miss a small piece of jewellery. He probably had chests full of trinkets. And their mother did need help. He was doing this for her.

It was a tight squeeze in the tunnel but the air was surprisingly fresh. Renni moved along, scraping his knees and elbows on the rough stone. A thick cobweb brushed against his face and something crawled up his sidelock. He hoped it wasn't a scorpion.

"Hurry up in there," Mahu's voice echoed from outside. "I think I can hear the *medjay* in the distance."

"I'm going as fast as I can," Renni called back, his voice bouncing off the walls.

Without warning, he bumped his head against a flat stone blocking his way. He nearly screamed with pain and shock. Then he pushed on it hard with both hands and it swung open like a flap, pitching him headfirst onto a sandy floor below.

Renni scrambled to his feet, spitting sand. The air was still rich with the smell of the incense and expensive spices that had been used in the general's burial ceremony. Moonlight filtered in from cracks in the ceiling, bouncing off a gold statue and illuminating a magnificent burial chamber. It was tightly packed with glittering things only a very wealthy and powerful person would have. A chariot stood on one side of the room, harnessed to a pair of wooden horses covered in gold leaf, reminding Renni of his father. Would his *ka* be looking down on him from the stars? If so, Renni hoped he'd understand it was mainly Mahu's idea to break into this tomb, not his.

A large umbrella with tassels hung over the chariot, as if the dead general was expecting to go riding in the hot sun. Next to it sat a cupboard covered in gemstones. There were golden dishes and washbowls. Enormous fans made with peacock feathers hung on the walls. Storage jars, no doubt filled with grain and beer for the deceased's afterlife, were piled up high against the wall. Four smaller jars sat in a neat row on another cupboard. Their lids where shaped like the four children of Horus and Renni knew they contained the stomach, intestines, lungs and liver of the dead general.

Renni shuddered and looked away to a golden boat carved all over with lotus flowers. On its narrow deck stood the mummies of cats, dogs and geese. They were the dead general's pets, waiting to travel with his *ka* to the stars.

The general's beautifully painted sarcophagus lay at the centre of the chamber. It was shaped like a man resting on his back, the hands holding a whip against the gold-encrusted chest. Two statues of foot soldiers stood by its feet while a statue of Anubis, the jackal-headed god and protector of the dead, loomed over its head.

Renni shivered. Being so close to a dead man made his skin crawl. He looked around for something he could steal without getting too close to the sarcophagus, but all the chests and cupboards were locked and even the dishes were too big to carry along the narrow tunnel. He had

no choice but to look in the sarcophagus itself.

Trying to ignore Anubis's steely glare, Renni pushed the heavy lid to one side. A sickly-sweet smell, like honey, rose out of the coffin. Renni could make out a bandaged head and a bloated hand that had broken free of the bandages. Slowly he reached in and felt around the mummy until his fingers touched something hard under the bandages. He grabbed it and the corpse's head turned sideways as he yanked it out. The bandages fell away, revealing the upper part of the general's face. His eyes snapped open and bore straight into Renni.

Renni screamed and jumped back, crashing into a statue of Hathor. Scrambling to his feet, he tightened his hold on his prize. He was shivering with terror. He needed to get out of the tomb fast, before fear drove him mad. Stuffing the stolen object under his belt, he used a gilded chair to reach the tunnel. Once inside it, he breathed a sigh of relief.

A spider crawled across his hand but he didn't even wince. It was nothing compared to the horror of looking a dead man in the eye.

"Did you find anything?" Mahu's voice floated down the tunnel.

"Yes! Just help me get out."

"Alright!" Mahu's powerful arms reached in and hauled Renni out. He leaned against the wall to catch his breath and brush cobwebs from his hair.

"Well," said Mahu. "What did you get?"

Rennie held out the object he'd snatched out of the sarcophagus. It was round and heavy and wrapped in a shiny white cloth.

The Heart Scarab
- Mahu -

Mahu snatched the object roughly. "Is this all you got?" he snapped. "It's a bit… small."

"It's the only thing I could get that would fit down the tunnel," said Renni defensively. "Everything else was locked away in chests or cupboards. It must be an amulet. Should be worth quite a few *deben*, I think."

Mahu peeled away the white cloth to reveal that Renni was right. The stolen object was an amulet. It was shaped like a scarab beetle, its wings folded tight against its body.

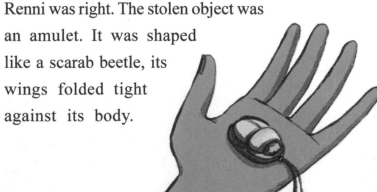

Amulets shaped like scarabs were as common as mosquitoes by the river. His mother had one but hers was made of stone and worth almost nothing. This one seemed to be made out of blue pottery called faience and the wings were covered in gold leaf. It should be worth something.

Mahu put the scarab carefully in his bag. "Help me place the stone back in the tunnel," he told Renni, glancing around him. "Your fear of being watched is getting to me. We shouldn't linger here."

With the entrance to the tunnel hidden once more, the two brothers parted. Renni went back to the small artists' village outside the Valley of the Kings and Mahu to his small fishing boat, hidden behind a rock.

A bright moon came out as Mahu pushed his boat away from the West Bank of the river. Now he was sure he was being followed. Twice he'd caught a glimpse of a head with unruly hair ducking behind rocks. "It's probably just a boy out poaching," Mahu assured himself. "But I'd better get away just the same."

Mahu was proud of his little boat, which he'd built himself out of papyrus reeds. He liked to think it was the sturdiest boat in his village. Even though he was officially a farmer, Mahu liked boats more than anything else in the world. His big dream was to work on one of them. *Imagine sailing away on a fine ship*, he often said to himself. *It would take you all the way to the sea, to fight with the pirates from the north.*

Mahu had been telling Renni the truth about needing to help their mother. But his dreams of sailing on the big, wide sea were the real reason he had forced his brother to break into the general's tomb. Many young men wanted to work on ships and a lad without connections would only get enlisted if he greased a captain's palm with an impressive gift. The plan was to trade the amulet for something a seafaring man would like. A beautifully carved wooden stool perhaps, which a sailor could use on deck. Or a seaman's chest made from precious acacia wood.

Mahu thought how smart he'd look wearing a sailor's clean kilt. Girls would flock to him. He'd marry well and get paid in sacks of wheat and beer. His mother would have enough to barter for anything she needed.

Approaching the East Bank, Mahu moored his skiff at a small jetty in Waset, the most glorious city in the Black Land. It was still the middle of the night so, using his bag as a pillow, he curled up in his skiff and went to sleep.

The sun was rising when Mahu woke up. Making sure his boat was securely tied, he left the riverbank and set off to the craftsmen's quarter. The streets were full of people on their way to market and the smell of baking hung in the air. Mahu's stomach growled with hunger but he had no time for food.

He crossed the busy marketplace and hurried

down a narrow street full of workshops. Most of them were already open, their doors set high in the wall to prevent sand from trickling in. Stopping outside a carpenter's shop, Mahu checked the amulet in his bag and hurried up a wooden ramp.

"Master Woodworker… Good morning," he said, parting a newly washed curtain.

A middle-aged man with curiously thick hair looked up from his pull-saw. "Can I help you?"

"I'm looking for a beautifully turned stool," said Mahu. "Or a seaman's chest."

The carpenter looked his young visitor up and down, his lips curled into a sneer. He was obviously not impressed by Mahu's homespun clothes.

"A farmer from one of the villages outside Waset, are you? What do you raise, dear? Sheep?"

Coming closer, Mahu realised the carpenter's unusually thick hair was really a wig made of dyed sheepskin. He fought the urge to say: *yes, and I might even have raised the one squatting on your head.*

Instead, he took out the general's amulet, holding it flat on his palm. "I have this to trade. Will it be enough to get a stool or a chest?"

The carpenter's eyes grew wide with amazement. "Where did you get that?"

"I inherited it from a rich uncle," lied Mahu. "A magnificent piece, isn't it?"

"A real treasure," whispered the carpenter. He reached out. "May I?"

Mahu dropped the amulet in his open hand. "By all means."

The carpenter moved over to a lamp, holding the amulet close to the light. He ran his fingers over the folded wings, admiring their shiny smoothness. "Truly, a remarkable piece of work."

He turned the amulet over and suddenly his eyes widened in horror. "Where did you say you got this?" he snapped at Mahu.

"I already told you. A rich uncle left it to me when he died."

The carpenter held out the amulet as if worried

it might be struck by lighting any moment. He was visibly trembling. "I can't accept this. How dare you bring such an object into my house? You could have dragged in all sorts of bad luck with you."

"It's just an amulet," protested Mahu.

"It's a heart scarab, you fool!" hissed the carpenter. "Look, the underside is covered in hieroglyphs. They are a sacred spell to help a dead person when Anubis weighs his heart against Ma'at's feather. Without it, the man's *ka* will not survive the judgement. This should be in a coffin, protecting its owner."

He handed Mahu the heart scarab back and spat at his feet. "Get out and don't you dare show your face in my workshop again or I'll report you to the *medjay*, you thief!"

3

A Waking Nightmare
- Renni -

Renni rubbed his eyes, trying very hard to stifle a yawn. After last night's misadventure, he'd found it impossible to sleep. Every noise outside the house had made him jump. He kept expecting the *medjay* to burst into his room with their dogs and trained monkeys.

"Renni," admonished Uncle Pepy. "What is the matter with you? I've had to correct your work three times already this morning. Are you unwell?"

"I'm alright, sir," said Renni. "Just a bit tired. This heat is getting to me."

Uncle Pepy frowned. "You're no good to me if

you can't work properly. Go find a quiet corner and have a short nap."

"Thank you, sir, I won't be long," replied Renni.

He washed his face at a bowl and hurried along a long, narrow corridor. Deeper in the tomb, the air was cooler. But finding a quiet spot to rest in was more difficult than he'd imagined. Every hall and chamber seemed to be noisy and crowded. He walked on until he came to a large hall with rough-hewn walls that still had to be decorated. It was dark. A light breeze blew in from some hidden crevice in the wall, disturbing the dust and sand on the floor.

Renni found a corner to sit in and wiped his face with his hands. Leaning back against the wall, he closed his eyes. He really was tired; his legs and arms felt as heavy as stone.

Strange, thought Renni. *I've never felt this tired in all my life...*

He became aware of strange voices murmuring in the dark.

He opened his eyes and peered around but could see no one. *It's just my imagination*, he thought. *I'm dreaming while still awake.*

The whispering got louder, echoing around the thick walls. A small, glowing flame appeared in the middle of the room, reminding Renni of the strange flickering lights he often saw among the papyrus reeds on the muddy banks of the river. Mahu said they were just glowing insects but others believed they were the *ka*s of people who had died with unfinished business. Was this flame one of them?

The breeze picked up, whipping up the sand on the floor. It whirled around Renni, growing stronger and stronger until it was a cold, shrieking wind. Sand danced around the light. The flame floated towards Renni, glowing brighter the closer it came. It grew in size too, getting wider and higher until it towered above him, a column of light. Renni clutched the amulet in his sidelock. "Horus, help me. Tawaret, goddess of protection, come to my aid."

The whirling sand and the light merged to form the shape of a man in loose robes. No—not robes. They were strips of white cloth, flapping around in the wind. Renni could see bits of papyrus covered in hieroglyphs fluttering out from between them. Gemstones and golden charms spilled out on the ground.

He was looking at a mummy.

The whispering turned into an angry, hissing voice. Now Renni could see two eyes glaring at him through the whirling sand. He recognised them at once. There was no mistaking them. They were the eyes of the dead general!

"You have stolen my heart scarab," snarled the general. "Soon Anubis will weigh my heart against the feather of Ma'at and I shall be judged by the forty-two gods of the Black Land. Without the spell inscribed on my heart scarab, I cannot utter the right incantation. I shall fail the test. My *ka* will be devoured by the monster Ammut."

"A heart scarab! I had no idea I was stealing a heart scarab," gasped Renni. "I thought it was just an ordinary pendant."

"Just an ordinary pendant indeed," thundered the dead general. "Everything in a coffin is sacred. You of all people, a painter of tombs, should know that."

The general hovered closer to Renni, enveloping him in his wildly flapping bandages. "But there may still be time to right the terrible wrong you have done. You must put my heart scarab back in my sarcophagus. And you must do it before the end of the Beautiful Festival of the Valley, when I will be summoned to face the jackal-headed god."

"I will, I promise," stuttered Renni. The mummy's eyes boring into him were making his head spin. The flying sand was making his eyes hurt.

"I warn you," echoed the general. "There is no escape from me. I will haunt you until you keep your word."

"I… I will return your heart scarab. I promise in the name of the gods." Renni could hardly get the words out. It felt like he was sinking in a sea of ground-up glass. He clawed at his throat, trying to breathe and then he passed out.

When he came round again, he was alone. There was no sand whirling around, no gemstones in the dust, no bits of papyrus. The dead general had vanished.

A figure appeared in the doorway. "Renni? Are you alright? You've been gone a while." It was Uncle Pepy.

"Did you see it?" gasped Renni. "The *ka*. There was a dead…"

Uncle Pepy shook his head firmly. "I saw only you thrashing on the floor. You must have had a nightmare. Come on, pull yourself together. The work manager's been asking where you are."

Renni got to his feet and followed his uncle out of the dark hall, back to the welcome noise of artists and stonemasons hard at work.

Uncle Pepy handed him a brush. "Fill in the reeds with green, and don't make any more mistakes. I want to finish this scene before we stop for the day."

Renni set to work, determined to concentrate on his painting. It wasn't easy. The dead general's last warning kept playing in his head.

I warn you. There is no escape from me. I will haunt you until you keep your word.

A Plague of Locusts
- Renni -

Renni hurried along the street where his mother and brother lived. It was early evening and children were playing with dolls and puppets on the doorsteps. The delicious smell of cooking wafted over the walls. It would soon be time for supper.

Renni's family home was on the outskirts of Waset, right on the edge of the desert. It was a poor district where working people lived and where the homes were small and tightly packed together. Renni's mother, Bu, like all her neighbours, was proud of her little mudbrick home and kept it as spotless as she could.

"Mother?" Renni pushed open the front door and stepped into a yard where his mother was baking.

"Son, is that you?" Renni's mother turned to the door, her face flushed from stoking up the outdoor oven. She was a small woman, with beautiful eyes and short hair that was turning grey. Renni thought how thin she looked in her baggy tunic that reached down to her ankles. Mahu was right. She was not eating enough.

"How nice to see you. Did my brother Pepy give you some time off?" Renni's mother touched the top of his head in blessing.

"Yes," said Renni. "But I can't stay too long. I have to be back in the artists' village by midnight." He handed his mother a bag of grain. "My wages, Mother."

"Thank you!" replied Mother. "It's lucky you came. I'm making your favourite cake: date and honey. You can take some back with you for Pepy."

She pushed aside a linen curtain to go indoors. "I'll get us some milk. Your brother will be with us shortly. He's gone to fetch water."

"Is he at the *shaduf*?" said Renni. "I'll go and help carry the jars. See you in a moment, Mother."

"Don't tell me you believe in ghosts," scoffed Mahu, hitching a water jar onto his shoulders.

"I'm telling you, the *ka* of the general appeared

to me," argued Renni, struggling to lift a second water jar. "It said I must return the heart scarab to his mummy, or else."

"Or else what?" laughed Mahu. "The dead general will come back to haunt you?"

"That's exactly what it told me," said Renni. "'*I will haunt you until you keep your word.*'"

"One man I tried to sell it to yesterday also said some rubbish about ghosts returning for their heart scarabs," said Mahu. "You all take this talk of gods and magic far too seriously. That pendant is just faience and gold, nothing more. There's nothing magical or mysterious about it. It's also the key to my future and I am not parting with it until I get what I want."

Renni held out his hand. "I insist you give it back. I want to return it tonight."

"You're wasting your time," tutted Mahu, turning to go. "I don't have it on me. It's hidden somewhere safe, where no one will find it. Now, are you gonna carry that second water jar or will

I have to come back for it myself?"

Renni lifted the jar to his shoulder. "I'll not stop asking until you give me the amulet," he shouted at his brother's back.

Mahu gasped and twitched, almost dropping his water jar. "Ouch! Something bit me on the chest."

"A bee?" said Renni.

"I said I was bitten not stung," replied Mahu. He turned and Renni saw a large, winged creature sitting on his brother's chest. It was green as a pam leaf, with small round eyes and hairy legs.

"It's only a locust," said Renni. "They don't bite."

"This one did," insisted Mahu. "Don't just stand there. Get it off me."

Renni was putting down his water jar when the locust took off, whirring up in the sky on its shimmering wings.

"I don't believe it," said Mahu, gazing up. "Little brother, look."

Renni looked up to see a dark shape forming in

the sky, a spiky cloud that seemed to billow with the wind.

"It's a whole swarm of locusts," shouted Mahu. "Forget the water jars. Run!"

"I don't think locusts attack people," said Renni.

But, a moment later, the swarm swooped down out of the sky. Spiky wings and little needle-sharp legs jabbed at Renni's face and arms. He flailed at the locusts with both hands but it was like swimming in thick honey. The harder he lashed out, the slower he moved.

"Help!" he tried to scream but the insects were fluttering against his face. And then, as if ordered by some unheard voice, the swarm rose as one back into the air. It flitted back and forth, billowing like a raincloud, and took the shape of a gigantic mummy. Soiled bandages fell away from the face to reveal two angry eyes that Renni had seen before.

"Remember my curse," roared the general, bending down so that the eyes brimming with fury

were looking straight into Renni's. "I will haunt you until you put the heart scarab back in my coffin. Hurry! Time is running out. The Beautiful Festival of the Valley is tomorrow night."

The mummy turned to glare at Mahu. "And you! You're the one who put your brother up to it. I know because my *ka* overheard your conversation outside my tomb. Do not think you shall go unpunished. If the monster Ammut devours my heart, I shall make sure she comes after you before you're even dead."

Danger on the River
- Mahu -

Mahu stood rooted to the spot, his eyes wide with horror. "Those weren't real locusts, where they? They were… magic. Nothing real disappears in an instant like that. And those horrible eyes…"

He shuddered and ran out of words. Only a short while ago, he'd been making fun of people who believed too much in gods and magic. Now… he was petrified.

"I told you," said Renni who was still trembling himself.

"You were right, little brother," said Mahu. "We've done something really stupid and we're going to pay a heavy price if we don't put it right immediately. We must return the heart scarab to the general at once. After supper, I'll tell Mother I'm taking you across the river on my boat and we'll break into the general's tomb on our way to the artists' village."

They hurried home with the water jars which they placed carefully inside the front door out of the reach of cats and insects. After the meal, Renni offered to wash the bowls.

"I'm taking Renni across the river, *Mut*," said Mahu. "It's getting late."

"Put on tunics, the both of you," replied his mother. "It's chilly tonight."

"Mine's on my bed," said Mahu. "I'll get it." He scurried up the ladder to the flat roof where his bed lay under a canopy. Taking only a moment to check the neighbour's children were fast asleep on the roof next door, he knelt on the floor and pulled out a small clay jar. He opened it and took out the heart scarab, which he hung around his neck. A moment later, he was back down in the yard and hugging his mother, the heart scarab hidden safely inside his tunic.

"Don't wait up for me, *Mut*," he said. "I'll let myself in when I get back."

He waited as Renni hugged his mother and she gave him her blessing. "May Hathor protect you. Come and see us again soon. And don't bring any more grain next time. Barter it for something nice for yourself. A new tunic, perhaps. This one is starting to look a bit shabby."

She thrust a little bag in his hands. "The rest of the cake for you and your uncle. Eat it before it goes stale."

"Thank you, *Mut*," said Renni. "I'll come and see you as soon as I can."

Mahu closed the front door behind them and they hurried to the riverbank. The moon had risen and a fine mist was blowing off the river.

Mahu hoped the *ka* of the dead general would not appear out of it. He could handle thieves, dishonest traders, even the *medjay* if he got into trouble but magic was something else. It scared him and that's why he'd always pretended he didn't believe in it. But now it had shown him its power, and he was terrified.

He couldn't wait to get rid of the heart scarab.

Mahu pushed his boat out in the water. The night fishermen had already left, hoping for a good catch of eel or catfish. He could see the lamps on their skiffs through the mist.

"Paddle hard," Mahu urged Renni. "And look out for crocodiles. It's hard to see them when it's this misty."

They reached the middle of the river without incident. The mist lifted and Mahu could see lights shining in the artists' village on the West Bank. *I'll soon get my little brother home safely*, he thought.

"Help! Please! In the name of the gods."

The shouting wrenched Mahu out of his thoughts.

Renni turned to him. "Someone's in trouble. Look!"

He pointed to a nearby fishing boat with lamps at the front and back. Someone was waving frantically from the prow.

"Help! I'm taking in water."

"Ignore him," said Mahu. "We don't want to be held up."

"But he might drown," argued Renni. "We can't leave him to the crocodiles."

"We're going the other way," insisted Mahu.

"He'll be heading to the East Bank."

Renni looked from his brother to the boat, which was listing heavily. "Let's just see if we can help him. A good deed might help the gods forgive us for breaking into a tomb."

"I suppose we do have a bit of time to spare," said Mahu, begrudgingly. They approached the bigger boat where the fisherman was reaching out. Up close, Mahu could see he was about his own age, with curly hair that hid most of his face. There was a strange scar that went around his neck; the kind you get when you accidentally touch hot metal. It almost looked like two snakes trying to eat each other.

"I've snagged my boat against something sharp," said the boy. "Have you any spare papyrus to plug the hole with?"

Renni turned to Mahu. "Have we any spare papyrus?"

"What fool would take to the water without it?" muttered Mahu. He reached to the front of the skiff where he kept a neat pile of tools and supplies. He handed a small roll of papyrus to Renni. "Here, you give it to the idiot."

"You do it," said the boy, trying to manoeuvre his boat closer. "I don't think the younger one can reach far enough."

"Very well," replied Mahu. He leaned over the side of the skiff. The boy reached out. His fingers brushed against the papyrus. Then, quick as lightning, he slapped Mahu's hand and sent it flying. His hand darted inside Mahu's tunic and closed around the heart scarab.

"Hey!" yelled Mahu, taken completely by surprise. He felt the strip of leather break against his neck and the boy leapt back in his boat, like a wild cat with its prize.

"Give it back!" shouted Mahu.

The boy only laughed and stepped further out of reach.

"I said give it back," insisted Mahu.

He was about to leap on the larger boat but the boy suddenly hurled a knife into the skiff. It pierced the bottom and water spurted in.

"The gods have pity on you," he sniggered. "Your little boat is taking in water. I'd try and plug the hole up if I were you. Assuming you have some more spare papyrus, that is." He started paddling away. "Pray to the gods the crocodiles don't get you. There's plenty of them in the river at this time of year, and they're always hungry."

PART 2

The old man peered into a basin filled with water that had been collected from the Great River at dawn, when magic was at its strongest. The surface was as smooth as a mirror. He could see his puppet, Abanoub, as though he were looking through an open window. The boy was sitting in a boat, clutching the general's heart scarab to his chest.

"Hold it up," he ordered. "Let me see it properly. I want to make sure it is the right one."

The old man's withered lips stretched into a grin as he peered at the heart scarab. He could see the general's name etched in the gold. It was certainly the right one. For a while, it had seemed that the magic amulet had slipped out of his grasp. He had instructed Abanoub to break into the general's tomb only to find the sarcophagus open, the heart scarab gone. But the boy had spotted the thieves and followed them. The old man had to admit Abanoub had shown great skill and initiative.

Perhaps he would reward him when he brought him the heart scarab.

"You have done well, boy," he said. "Heka is pleased with you."

Abanoub nodded. "Thank you, master." He could hear the old man's voice echoing in his head like the remnant of a dream after the dreamer wakes up.

"Bring the amulet to my house," commanded the old man. "I shall give you directions. Don't fail me at the last hurdle now."

The old man looked up at the statue of Heka. "Thank you, my lord," he whispered. "The heart scarab is almost mine. My revenge on my enemy will soon be complete. And then I shall deal with those two young thieves most severely. I will unleash all the powers of your magic against them."

6

The Princess Balaal

- Renni -

Renni sighed with relief as he and Mahu finished patching up the skiff. They'd been very lucky. No crocodiles had appeared while they dragged their damaged boat onto the riverbank.

"What happens now?" he asked.

"We'll have to go after the thief," replied Mahu.

Renni was uncertain. "Uncle Pepy will fire me if I'm not back by midnight. I might already be late."

"You go home then," said Mahu through gritted teeth. "I'll hunt the thief down myself."

Renni hesitated. He couldn't leave his brother to chase the thief alone. They were family after all, and the gods liked families sticking together. Besides, the idea that he might be haunted by the *ka* of the dead general for the rest of his life if he failed filled Renni with dread. "I'll come with you," he said. "But how are we going to find the thief?"

"We can start by going in the same direction he did," replied Mahu. "There'll be two of us paddling and only one of him. We'll catch up with him in no time."

They pushed the repaired skiff away from the riverbank and started paddling. Now that the mist had melted, a bright moon shone on the river, turning it silver. The sky was bejewelled with stars. Renni looked out for the dog star: the place where some of the gods lived. He hoped they were looking down on him and Mahu. Would they be angry with them for breaking into a tomb, Renni wondered, or pleased that they were trying hard to repair the damage they had done?

"Hey, Renni. Look!" Mahu pointed with his

paddle at the water. A dark shape was forming around the skiff, clearly visible in the moonlight.

"They're small fish," said Mahu. "Hundreds of them. I've seen them making shoals like this before but never around a moving boat."

The dark shoal swirled, like the shadow of a tree in the wind. It changed shape, stretching and widening till it took the shape of a gigantic man lying prone on the water. The image lasted only a moment but

Renni had no doubt that it had been there.

"Did you see it?" he asked Mahu.

His brother nodded.

"Do you think it was the general?" he whispered.

"If it is," said Mahu, "I don't think he means to scare us this time. Look!"

The fish had regrouped, forming a new shape in front of the boat. It looked like an arrow.

"Perhaps the general is telling us to follow them," said Renni.

"The thief went the other way," replied Mahu. "They're pointing in the wrong direction."

"He might have turned back without us noticing," said Renni. "I think we should trust the magic. I think the general is trying to help us."

"Very well," said Mahu. They turned the boat round and followed the arrow in the water. It led them on past the houses of the rich with pontoons on the river, past the great temples of Hathor and Amun-Ra, and then along long stretches of neat orchards full of date palms.

"What's that ahead?" said Renni as the river widened and the banks on either side grew distant.

"It's an island," replied Mahu. "Crocodile Island! I've been here once to visit a friend. Perhaps the dead general wants us to consult with her."

"Who is she?" asked Renni.

"She often comes to the market to barter for vegetables," said Mahu. "She invited me to a party once."

"What does she barter?"

"You'll see," said Mahu as they paddled closer to the island and the fish in front of the boat scattered. Renni hopped out to moor the skiff, disturbing a family of ducks sleeping in the reeds.

"That quacking will have warned everyone we're here," said Mahu. "Stay close to me. The people on this island don't trust strangers, so let me do the talking."

They pushed their way through the papyrus and found themselves outside a crumbling building half-buried in the sand. A large window that now served as a doorway stood in front of them. There was a crocodile carved in the stone above it.

"Is this a forgotten temple?" gasped Renni.

Mahu nodded. "Dedicated to Sobek, the crocodile god. The priests abandoned it a long time ago, and the shifting sands from the river have almost buried it. But that's proved quite handy for some. You'll see in a moment."

Renni was full of questions as he followed his brother through the window and down a rope into a large hall. Statues of crocodiles standing on their hind legs glared at him. Their mouths were open to show sharp teeth and pointed tongues. He shuddered.

Crocodiles scared him. He could never be a follower of Sobek, even though the god was believed to protect the Nile and Pharaoh.

Renni could hear the muffled sound of people talking as Mahu led him down a narrow corridor and into a second, smaller hall. This one had little cubbyholes, each one containing a small, mummified crocodile.

"This bit of the temple is a necropolis, isn't it?" he whispered. "An underground graveyard for crocodiles."

Mahu grinned. "And the idea of so many dead crocodiles all in one place keeps most people away from the island."

The chattering voices grew clearer as he led Renni down yet another narrow corridor and into a small round room where a fire was burning in a shallow bowl. Several children were sitting around it, toasting huge slabs of bread on the end of pointed sticks.

One of them scrambled to his feet, placing a crutch under his left shoulder. He was a very small boy, with a dimple in his chin and bright green eyes.

"State your name and the reason for your visit," he said.

Mahu gave his name. "And this is my brother Renni. We are looking for Balaal."

The boy looked him up and down. "Are you her friend, the farmer? She's mentioned you. You let us have some onions one winter when we had nothing else to eat. We'll always be grateful."

He pointed at a narrow doorway with his crutch. "She's through there."

Renni and Mahu hurried out of the circular

room. "You let those children have some onions?" said Renni. "When was this?"

"Last year," replied Mahu. He grinned. "But I didn't let them have any of *my* onions. I can't afford to give away anything. I just showed them a field that belongs to a rich farmer."

"You're a rascal," said Renni.

They reached another room, with brightly coloured walls painted to show the gods and goddesses of Kemet. A huge statue of Sobek, the crocodile-headed god, stood behind a broken altar. A fire burned in a bowl in front of it, throwing eerie shadows on the walls so that the painted gods looked as if they were alive and moving.

A girl emerged from the shadows. She was beautiful, with enormous dark eyes and thin eyebrows. Her long, thick hair flowed down around her shoulders.

"Who seeks the oracle of the crocodile god?" she said in a deep voice. Then she seemed to recognise Mahu because her eyes lit up. "Mahu," she cried in a normal girl's voice. "How nice to see you. I knew you'd pay me a visit again."

"Did the gods tell you that?" Mahu asked.

"Don't be silly," said the girl. "I only act as the oracle on important matters."

"This is my brother Renni," said Mahu. He nudged Renni forward. "Bow to the girl. She is a runaway princess."

"My proper title is Princess Balaal, first daughter of He Who Reigns in the City of the Sea," explained the girl. "But my close friends just call me Balaal." She held out a hand. "You can call me that too."

Renni bent to kiss the princess's hand but she pulled it back quickly and laughed.

"I was only joking. A true princess does not need to have her hand kissed. She knows she is true royalty from the moment she is born."

"Balaal comes from the land of the Fenkhu," explained Mahu.

"I am not a fugitive from justice," said Balaal.

"My father sent me to safety because there are rebels who would like to destroy our family and take power in our land."

"Balaal could buy her own palace if she wanted to," explained Mahu. "She could have guards and servants to look after her every need, but she prefers to live with the homeless children on Crocodile Island."

"My father's enemies would find me right away if I lived in a palace," said Balaal. "Besides the children here need me." She smiled at Renni. "Your brother is very proud of you. He told me you are an artist."

"I am still a *sesh qedut*," replied Renni humbly. "But I hope to work in the grand temples when I grow up."

"You people of the Black Land love grand temples," she said. She turned to Mahu. "How can I help you?"

"A boy stole an amulet from us," said Mahu. "We want to find him and take it back." He looked at Renni. "If we need her help, we're going to have to tell her the truth."

"I take it you have committed a crime yourselves then," said Balaal.

Mahu nodded. "We stole the heart scarab from a tomb and we have to return it by the end of the Beautiful Festival of the Valley tomorrow. If we don't, the man we stole it from will not pass Anubis's test. His heart will be devoured by Ammut, the monster of darkness."

"And the *ka* of the dead man will come after us," added Renni. "The boy who stole it from us is a fisherman. We don't know where to find him."

"I shall consult the gods and find out where he is," said Balaal.

"You're speaking to Sobek?" asked Renni.

"No," said Balaal. "The gods of the Black Land only answer simple questions with a yes or a no. I shall consult my own goddess, Astoreth; she speaks from the beyond."

She put on a thin veil to cover her face. "Stand

on the other side of the altar if you want to watch. But, whatever happens, don't interrupt me."

She threw a heavy cloth over the statue of Sobek to hide the god's face. Then she added twigs and herbs to the fire on the altar, making the flames leap. Opening a jar, she scattered white powder. A thick sheet of silvery smoke rose from the fire. Renni could see Balaal's face reflected in it, eyes drawn wide, her hair standing in a halo around it.

A strange, bird-like noise rose from Balaal's lips. Renni's skin crawled. He was a firm believer in the gods of the Black Land and this connection with deities from strange lands made him uneasy. Would the great Hathor and Isis be offended that he was seeking the help of a foreign goddess? Would Sobek be angry that he had allowed someone to cover his face in his own temple? He hoped not.

The fire in the bowl died. The silvery smoke disappeared. Balaal removed her veil.

"The goddess has spoken to me," she said. "The

boy who stole your amulet is being controlled by someone very powerful. Astoreth tells me we shall find him at the great temple of Amun-Ra."

"Then we must go there at once," said Mahu. He turned to Renni. "Come on, little brother. Back to the skiff. We have no time to lose."

"I shall come with you," said Balaal. "The goddess also told me you will need my help."

In the Temple of Amun-Ra
- Mahu -

The sun hadn't yet risen by the time Mahu, Renni and Balaal reached the outskirts of Waset. They hid the skiff behind a boulder. Then they made their way on foot along the banks of the Great River. It was the day of the Beautiful Festival of the Valley and people from all over the Black Land were arriving in droves. They all seemed to be heading towards Nesut-Towi, the temple complex of Amun-Ra, where free food and drink would be available in the vast courtyard behind the enclosure walls.

"It's going to be very difficult spotting the thief in this crowd," said Renni. "I might not even recognise him. We only saw him for a few moments, in the dark of night."

"Don't worry, I never forget a face," Mahu assured him. "I'd recognise the villain anywhere."

"But when we find him, how are we getting the heart scarab off him?" asked Renni.

"Patience, little brother," said Mahu. "We shall solve that problem when we get to it."

As they approached the temple, the crowds got even thicker and noisier. They reminded Mahu of the river after the floods, when the powerful waters rise to overflow the banks, sweeping everything before them. There were *medjay* everywhere in case the crowds got out of control. Fights often broke out over free food during festivals, leaving people dead or injured.

Renni is right, Mahu thought. *It's going to be very difficult finding the thief in this tide of people.*

He scanned the crowds and caught sight of a lone figure pushing their way through the sea of people: a boy, who stood out from the rest

because of his stooped shoulders and the annoyed expression on his face. He was the only fish swimming against the current, trying to make his way past the temple gate rather than towards it.

"There's our thief," gasped Mahu. "Come on."

The three set off after the lone boy. They turned a corner past a second gate and then a third where the crowds seemed to be thinner. The thief started to walk faster.

"Hurry up, let's not lose him," said Mahu.

"I think he's making for the city centre," said Balaal.

And then a noblewoman nearby started screaming. She was wearing a fine linen robe with a jewelled collar around the neck. On her head was a wig big enough to make a vulture's nest. "Help! Someone has stolen my golden fan. Help!"

Immediately, the noblewoman was surrounded by her bodyguards: tall men with powerful arms and sharp swords. *Medjay* pushed their way through the crowds, brandishing their spears.

"Don't worry, ma'am," said one of them. "We'll search the crowd until we find your fan."

He bellowed at the crowds. "Everyone, stop where you are. Don't move until I say you can."

The boy who had stolen the heart scarab stopped right outside the temple gate. He cocked his head sideways, as if listening to some invisible friend speaking to him, then slipped unnoticed through the gate.

"He's worried the *medjay* might search him and find the heart scarab," said Mahu. "He's going to hide in the temple. After him, quick!"

"But the *medjay* told us not to move," said Renni.

"Don't worry. They got the fan thief, look," cut in Balaal, pointing to a girl who was being dragged away by the *medjay*. "Let's go."

As the crowd started to move again, the three elbowed their way into the great courtyard. Mahu saw the heart scarab thief hurrying up the steps to the main inner temple in the enclosure, the temple of Amun-Ra himself.

"The *medjay* at the door will never let him in," said Mahu. "Only priests and royalty are allowed inside the temples."

"And artists," added Renni. "They're allowed in too, but only to paint before the temple is finished."

But even as he spoke, the thief slipped unnoticed past the *medjay*.

"There's something strange going on with that boy," said Balaal. "I think there's magic involved. He sneaked into that temple like a wisp of smoke."

"Spooky," said Renni.

Balaal laughed. "No spookier than a couple of boys haunted by the ghost of a dead general, if you ask me. Come on. Let's go after that boy before we lose him for good."

"But how will *we* get into the inner temple?" asked Mahu.

Balaal did not reply. Instead she marched up

to the *medjay* at the door and held up her hand to show a large ring on her middle finger. It had a purple stone with a seal carved in it.

The medjay both clicked their heels together and bowed. "Welcome to the temple of Amun-Ra, your highness."

"I come to pay homage to the gods of the Black Land," said Balaal as one of the guards pulled a curtain aside. "Please make sure my attendants and I are left undisturbed until we come out again."

Mahu was full of admiration for Balaal as he followed her into the temple. Her brazen cheek worked every time. He had seen her use it at the market to charm people into giving her things she needed for the homeless children. It was the reason he admired her so much. Glancing at Renni, he noticed his brother, however, was very uneasy. Perhaps he was afraid of entering a temple on false pretences. Mahu put a hand on his shoulder to reassure him.

The curtain fell into place, plunging the temple

into near darkness. Mahu peered around him. The air was heavy with incense but he could see rows of thick columns that rose up into the darkness. At the far end of the temple, a colossal statue showed Amun-Ra sitting on a throne.

The thief was hurrying towards it.

"You! Thief!" shouted Mahu. "Hand over the heart scarab!"

The boy stopped between the statue's gigantic feet. Once again he cocked his head sideways as if listening to instructions. A sly grin spread across his face. He pulled the heart scarab out from under his belt and held it out towards Mahu. It caught the light from a lamp hanging above the statue, making it twinkle like a star.

"Is this what you're after?" he hissed. Then his laugh echoed around the empty temple. He stepped sideways... and vanished.

8

The Sea of Snakes
- Renni -

"There *is* magic involved!" gasped Balaal. "Your Amun-Ra made the boy vanish into thin air."

"I'm afraid it's not magic this time," said Renni. "I've helped Uncle Pepy in enough temples to know that the boy just escaped through a secret door. A lot of temples and palaces have them. The priests use them to pretend they can vanish and reappear at will. They always lead into a secret tunnel."

He pointed to a door painted inside the statue's left foot. "That's what we call a false door. They're meant to be a symbol to show communication between gods and men. Most of the time they're just a picture of a door. But sometimes, they are real."

He stepped up to the door, peered at the hieroglyphs around the doorframe and pressed one of them. The door slid open, revealing narrow steps.

"Great work, little brother," said Mahu, impressed.

The three of them stepped through the false door and it closed smoothly behind them. The steps wound deep into the ground, leading into a narrow corridor. Holding out his hands, Renni could feel hieroglyphs carved in the walls. They spelled curses on people who trespassed into the tunnel without a good reason.

Finding the heart scarab is a good reason, he kept telling himself. *Please don't curse us. We're saving the dead general from the jaws of Ammut.*

It soon became clear that the winding corridor was a maze. With rising panic, Renni realised they were lost.

"I wish I'd thought to bring a light," muttered Balaal. "But then who'd have guessed we'd end up in an underground tunnel?"

Suddenly an idea crossed Renni's mind. "I've just remembered a trick Uncle Pepy once taught me," he said. "In case I ever got lost in an underground tomb."

"And do you often get lost in underground tombs?" joked Balaal.

"Leave the poor boy alone," said Mahu. "Teasing him is my job. What's the trick, little brother?"

"You lick your forefinger," explained Renni, wetting his finger. "Then you hold it out like you're pointing at something. If you stand still, you'll feel a very faint breeze on your fingertip, and you walk into it because the breeze will be blowing in from the end of the tunnel." He held out his finger. "Do you feel it?"

"It's true," said Mahu, after he'd licked his forefinger and held it out. "I can definitely feel the wind on my finger. Follow me, everyone."

The three of them followed Mahu along the corridor, Renni silently thanking the gods for reminding him about Uncle Pepy's trick. They turned several more corners but never came up against another dead end. At last, they ducked through a low doorway and found themselves in a tunnel with sunlight shining at the far end. Renni heaved a sigh of relief. He could smell the clean scent of the river!

"We're nearly there," he said, taking the lead.

But Mahu grabbed him by the tunic and pulled him back roughly. "Careful, little brother."

"Yes, listen," said Balaal. "I can hear hissing."

Renni listened. Mahu and Balaal were right. There *was* a hissing sound and it was rising from the floor. Renni looked down to see an open pit crawling with large snakes. Their heads were raised and their hoods were open. His heart turned to ice.

"Cobras!"

There must have been hundreds of them, a sea of slithering scaly bodies and flicking tongues. The floor of the pit was littered with skulls and human bones.

"How do we get to the other side of the pit?" he said. "It stretches from wall to wall. There's no way round."

"I could try leaping across," said Mahu.

Renni shuddered at the thought. "Please don't. You might fall in."

"We don't have to jump," said Balaal. "We could *dance* across the pit. My people are famous for their sacred Snake Dance."

"You can't be serious," gasped Renni.

"Watch and listen," replied Balaal. She started humming a strange tune, the sound vibrating deep in her chest. Kneeling at the edge of the pit, she raised her arms and waved her hands slowly. The snakes followed her waggling fingers with their beady eyes, their tongues flicking rapidly. They seemed to be transfixed. The princess reached down into the pit, allowing a cobra to wind itself around each arm and slither up to her elbows.

Then she stepped carefully down into the pit and started dancing, picking her way expertly around the snakes, her arms high above her head.

"Quick, dance behind me," she hissed at Renni and Mahu. "Have courage. The snakes won't hurt you while the sacred spell lasts. Listen, they've gone all silent." She resumed her humming and the snakes on the floor swayed and undulated around her.

"Come on, little brother," whispered Mahu. "Have faith in yourself. You can do this."

He stepped into the pit after Balaal. Renni, though, just couldn't follow him. He remained on the edge, frozen with terror.

"Come on, Renni," urged Mahu, turning to his brother.

Summoning up his courage, Renni managed to dip one toe in the pit only to pull it out again as if he'd been scalded with boiling water. The sudden movement made the snakes hiss again. They turned as one towards Renni, their jewel-like eyes unblinking.

"I can't do it," he tried to whisper but fear had silenced his voice completely.

Balaal sang louder and waved her arms with the cobras around them. The snakes on the floor turned their heads and fixed their glassy eyes on her again. They were back under her spell.

Mahu, who'd reached the centre of the pit, picked his way back to Renni. "I'll carry you across. Trust me, little brother." His powerful hands closed around Renni's waist and he lifted him onto his shoulders. "Close your eyes and don't open them until I tell you. We'll soon be on the other side."

Slowly, the two brothers made their way through the sea of snakes. His eyes firmly shut, Renni prayed to all the gods he could think of. And he thanked them for giving him such a brave, caring brother.

"We're there, Renni," he heard Mahu say. He opened his eyes to see Balaal climbing out of the pit. Mahu let Renni scramble up behind her. He lay on the floor, catching his breath. "Thank you, Mahu," he said. "I shall never forget this."

Mahu smiled, climbing out of the pit. "It's what big brothers are for."

Balaal lowered her arms into the snake pit and let the two cobras crawl down. "And we must thank the goddess Astoreth too. It was her snake dance that saved us."

"Yes," agreed Renni. "We thank Astoreth too."

Mahu got to his feet, dusting his tunic and loincloth. "Come on. I can hear people in the distance. We're nearly there."

A pained moaning caught their attention. Renni spotted someone lying in the tunnel's mouth. He was framed by the bright light outside and there was no mistaking that unruly, curly hair.

It was the heart scarab thief.

Mahu sprinted towards him. The thief was

shaking violently. As Renni, Mahu and Balaal approached, Renni could see he was covered in sweat. His lips had turned a dark blue. He'd been bitten by a cobra.

"Serves you right," growled Mahu. The thief had hung the heart scarab around his neck. Mahu tore it off.

"Let me attend to him, Mahu," said Balaal. "He only has moments to live unless I remove the poison immediately."

"Leave him to die," said Mahu, hanging the heart scarab around his own neck. "He caused a lot of trouble. He deserves it."

"Let Balaal save him, Mahu," said Renni. "We're guilty of stealing the heart scarab too, and I don't think we deserve to die."

"Fine!" Mahu stepped aside to let Balaal kneel by the dying boy. Gently, she pulled the sides of the snakebite apart with her thumbs, letting the blood flow out. The thief shook and howled in pain. His eyes rolled upwards so that only the whites were visible.

"He made me do it," he gasped through clenched teeth. "He made me steal the heart scarab. He was guiding me through the snake pit only the hissing was so loud, I couldn't hear the instructions."

"Who made you do it?" asked Renni.

"The old man in the palace. He controls me with his dark magic. My name is Abanoub. I am just his puppet."

"But who *is* he?" asked Renni.

"His great highness," came back the stuttered reply. "Pharaoh's very own vizier."

PART 3

The vizier muttered furiously as he peered into his basin of magic water. He could see Renni and Mahu bent over Abanoub. There was a third person with them, a girl he'd never seen before. She was trying to help the thief.

He caught sight of the heart scarab around Mahu's neck. Curse those children! The pain from the snakebite had been so painful, he had lost control of Abanoub. And the children had won.

But wait! Peering closer, the vizier could see the girl bending over Abanoub. She put her mouth to the snakebite and sat up. Turning away from the boys, she spat the poison against the wall.

Abanoub went limp but Renni held his head while the girl removed more of the poison.

"He's out of danger now," she said after she'd spat out poison four or five times.

The vizier passed his curved wand over the basin to make his magic more powerful. "Boy, wake up," he growled. "Your master commands it."

Slowly, Abanoub's eyes flickered open. He could hear his master's voice inside his head again, loud and clear. His real self melted away, like a strip of fog in morning sunshine. He was back under the vizier's control.

"Do not speak," instructed the vizier. "Just do as I tell you."

A wicked grin played on his withered lips as he growled his instructions. He watched Abanoub totter to his feet, pretend to lean on Mahu for support... and then grab the heart scarab.

"The magic of Heka give your legs strength and speed," roared the vizier. "Run!"

And Abanoub sprinted out of the tunnel.

9

The Vizier's Palace
- Mahu -

Renni stared dumbfounded after the running Abanoub. "What just happened?"

"The rascal tricked us," said Mahu. "Come on, after him. We haven't a moment to lose."

The three of them ran out of the tunnel and found themselves on the famous avenue of sphinxes. They could hardly move in the crowd and they soon lost sight of Abanoub.

"Don't worry," said Renni. "Did the boy not say his master was Pharaoh's vizier? He must be heading towards his house. We'll follow him there."

"But do either of you know where the vizier

lives?" asked Balaal.

"Everyone knows where the vizier lives," replied Mahu. "He's one of the most famous people in our country."

"And rumour has it that he is the secret high priest of magic," added Renni. "He is a follower of Heka. I'm not surprised he has the power to control people."

"Then we must go to the vizier's house and get the amulet back," said Mahu.

He shaded his eyes and looked up at the sky. It was late afternoon. They had a few hours left before the sun set. And just a few hours more before midnight, when the dead general had to face Anubis…

"That's the vizier's grand residence," said Mahu. He, Balaal and Renni were hiding in an orchard across the street from the vizier's house.

"It is almost as big as my father's palace," said

Balaal. "The vizier must be incredibly rich and powerful."

"It is said he can turn rocks into solid gold," commented Renni.

"That's only a stupid rumour," said Mahu.

"But how are we going to get inside?" asked Balaal. "The place must be crawling with servants and slaves."

"I have an idea," said Mahu. "But first we need a basket, and some fruit from this orchard." He turned to Renni. "Can you go get one? I saw a woman bartering baskets just down the road. Don't be long. We haven't much time."

"I'll go. I'm good at trading," said Balaal. While she set off to the market, Mahu and Renni explored the orchard. It seemed to be abandoned. Most of the trees needed a good pruning but their branches were heavy with fruit. Mahu and Renni's arms were soon full of figs, peaches and overripe pomegranates.

When Balaal returned, she was carrying a large basket. "I bartered it for one of my rings," she said. "The woman at the stall couldn't believe her luck when I told her I had nothing less valuable!"

"You were very generous," said Renni. "Thank you."

Balaal smiled. "There are more precious things in the world than silver jewellery. Now what's your big plan, Mahu?"

"I want you both to hide behind the sphinxes on either side of the vizier's gate," he replied. "While I create a diversion with this basket of fruit, I want you to slip inside the grounds and hide. I'm sure the vizier and most of the household will leave for the Beautiful Festival of the Valley soon. When the coast is clear, you must open the gate and let me in. We'll find the heart scarab together."

Renni and Balaal nodded, then ran across the street and hid behind the marble sphinxes, one on either side of the door. Mahu waited to make sure they were well out of sight before crossing the street himself. He climbed the stairs to the vizier's gate and knocked loudly, whistling confidently.

The gate opened and Hotep, the vizier's head slave, looked out. He was already dressed for the festival, with a gleaming necklace round his neck and many rings flashing on his fingers. His robe was so white, it made Mahu's eyes hurt. "Can I help you, young man?" he asked.

"I come bearing a gift for his highness," said

Mahu, holding out the basket. "To honour the vizier's dead relatives on the day of the festival."

"A gift you say?" Hotep turned up his nose at the plain basket and dusty fruit.

"From my humble master, who wishes to remain anonymous," said Mahu brazenly. "Someone lowly at Pharaoh's court who the vizier helped in his time of need. The fruit might not look like much, but it has been blessed by a priestess of Isis. They are now sacred. Look, I have figs, the symbol of thankfulness, and peaches, which represent kindness. And my master has sent pomegranates too, in case his highness suffers from tapeworm in the stomach."

Mahu gave the head slave his brightest smile. It always worked on girls and grannies and he hoped it might work on this wrinkly old man too.

"I shall call someone to take it," said Hotep.

He turned to call one of the lesser slaves.

"Oh, you don't need to bother any of his highness's staff," said Mahu hurriedly. "They'll

all be busy getting ready for the festival. I'll just put the basket inside the gate."

He climbed the last step and pretended to miss his footing. The basket flew out of his hands and fruit went rolling down the steps.

"You careless fool," growled Hotep. "Pick them up before someone slips on them. And don't squash any pomegranates under your big feet. They'll stain the marble."

He stepped out of the gate to chase after the fruit, wincing in pain as he tried to bend down. The moment gave Renni and Balaal the chance to slip inside.

"I am sorry for my clumsiness, sir," said Mahu, picking up the escaped fruit. He handed the basket to Hotep. "Here, you take it before I cause any damage. Have a good festival."

Hotep glared as Mahu disappeared down the street, whistling loudly.

"Children nowadays," he muttered. "They have absolutely no respect."

10

Talgu
- Renni -

Hiding behind a small shrine in the garden, Renni and Balaal saw Hotep marching up to the main house with their basket. Loud, excited chatter echoed out of the windows. It seemed Mahu was right. The entire household was going to the festival.

After a while, Hotep appeared at the door and clapped twice. Two slaves, in gold-embroidered tunics came round the corner carrying an empty sedan chair, a sort of throne on two poles. A man in a shiny wig—Renni recognised him as Paser, the

famous vizier—emerged from the house and was helped into it. Two young women with large fans made of peacock feathers stationed themselves on either side of it. The vizier would not arrive at the festival hot and sweaty.

The rest of the household formed a procession, young ones in front of the sedan chair, the older slaves behind it, all armed with harps and tambourines. Hotep came out of the house last of all, carrying a staff topped with the vizier's symbol—a jackal.

He tapped the ground three times and the procession set off, leaving a house guard to lock the gate behind it. Renni and Balaal watched from their hiding place to see what the guard would do next. He sat in the sun for a while, yawning and scratching his tummy. Then someone called him from the servant's quarters on the other side of the house.

"Abrax! Your lunch is ready."

As soon as the guard disappeared, Renni hurried to the gate, drew the bolt and Mahu slipped in.

"We're going to have to be really careful," Renni warned him as he locked the gate again. "Not everyone has gone to the festival with the vizier. There's still guards and servants in their quarters."

"Don't worry," said his brother. "Guards and servants are no match for wily old Mahu. Let's find a way into the main house. I'm sure the heart scarab will be hidden somewhere in the vizier's private quarters."

They tried the front door but it was securely locked. The back door, which the servants who worked in the kitchen used for carrying in food supplies and throwing out the rubbish, was also barred. The windows were all shuttered securely.

"There has to be a way in," said Mahu.

"There is," said Balaal. She indicated a grapevine growing against the back wall. Led by Mahu, the three clambered up the gnarled trunk and found themselves on a sumptuous roof terrace. There was a large bed under an awning with a beautifully made cabinet next to it. Enormous pots were dotted around, each one overflowing with fragrant flowers. This was the vizier's summer bedroom. He could lie on the bed and enjoy the marvellous views of the Great River and the desert.

"There's a way in, look," said Renni.

He pushed an embroidered curtain aside. The others followed and made their way along a wide corridor with palm trees painted on the walls. At the far end was a second curtain that opened into a bathroom. It had an enormous bath and a statue of Hapi, the god of the river, standing above it. A third curtain led them into the room they were looking for. The vizier's dressing chamber.

All three looked around them in disbelief. There were enough clothes to dress an entire court. Wigs were perched on wooden heads, each one more extravagant than the next. A dressing table was covered in tubs of makeup and perfume bottles.

"And here's a jewellery box," said Balaal.

"More like a jewellery chest," said Renni. "It's enormous."

Balaal opened it carefully to reveal a set of drawers, all crammed full of treasures. But there was no sign of the heart scarab.

"He has taken it with him to the festival," croaked an unfamiliar voice.

They all turned to see a woman who had crept up on them unnoticed. She was bent double with age but her eyes were full of fire.

"Please, don't call the guards," Renni said. "We only want the heart scarab because…"

"Because we want to return it to its rightful owner," cut in Balaal quickly.

The woman smiled. "They call me Talgu, on account of my white hair. I used to be head cook once. Now they say I am old and soft in the head, only good to clean dead lotus leaves out of the pool or to sweep the floor. They think because I am weak in body, I am also weak in mind. But ancient Talgu sees everything, even things that are meant to be secret." She tapped her nose. "Ancient Talgu knows everything…"

"And you say the vizier took the heart scarab to the festival?" said Mahu.

Talgu nodded. "It is hidden inside his tunic. I watched him put it on. You must go to the festival yourselves if you want it."

"Why are you telling us this?" asked Renni. "Why are you helping us?"

A sad look appeared in Talgu's eyes. "I am a

grandmother. It is not right what the master is doing to that poor boy, controlling him like that, making him steal. He's just a child, some poor woman's son."

"Thank you, Talgu." Renni bowed to the old woman as a sign of respect. "We'll try and help Abanoub if we can."

"It seems we'll have to face the vizier at the festival," said Balaal.

"And we must hurry," added Mahu. "Who knows what he is planning?"

11

The Beautiful Festival of the Valley
- Mahu -

By the time Renni, Mahu and Balaal joined the crowds on the riverbank and found their skiff, the statues of Amun-Ra, his wife Mut and their son Khonsu had been carried out of their temples and on to the royal barge. It was to cross the river to the West Bank where the gods would bless the dead pharaohs in their tombs. Large crowds followed them, strewing flowers in their way and holding up painted images of their dead relatives.

Despite the joyous music, the dancing and the delicious food, the Beautiful Festival of the Valley was a celebration of the dead. People wanted to show their dear departed ones that they still remembered them and treasured their memories.

As Pharaoh boarded the barge with the vizier and his retinue, the crowds cheered and held up bunches of flowers to be blessed by the gods. Later they would lay them on the graves of their dead relatives.

Pharaoh was a tall, handsome man with kind eyes and red hair tucked under the double crown of the Black Lands. He made the wizened old vizier who stood beside him look like a drooling vulture, all bones and beady eyes. *How could someone who looked like he might die any moment be so dangerous*, Mahu wondered.

"Do you know what the people of the Black Land call Pharaoh?" Renni said to Balaal, eager to show his knowledge of the Black Land's culture. "Keeper of the Harmony and Balance, Strong in Right, Elect of Amun-Ra. They say his hair is not dyed. It really is flaming red. His beard is stuck on though. It shows that he is a god. We always paint him like that in pictures."

"Now's not the time to talk about hair dye, little brother," said Mahu. "It's time we tried getting our hands on the heart scarab. We need to get into my skiff and follow the royal barge across the river."

Mahu's skiff was not the only one following the royal barge and the statues of the gods. This was the only time of year ordinary people could set foot on the West Bank, the Land of the Dead, without fear of punishment from both the law and the gods. The river was heaving with boats and punts.

"We have no chance of getting close to the vizier on water," said Balaal. "We'll try when we get to the West Bank."

"I think it'll be easier if I go on my own," said Mahu. "You two wait for me in the skiff."

On the other side of the river, they found the boats were moored four lines deep. Mahu had to jump from one to another to reach the riverbank.

"Mahu, be careful," Renni called out after him.

Mahu held up a hand to show he would be alright, then turned and disappeared in the crowd.

But he soon realised that getting close to the royal party was going to be difficult. The priests and *medjay* formed a tight ring around it, like a wall defending a fort. The *medjay* were on high alert. The sharp points on their spears caught the fading sunlight, and Mahu knew they would not hesitate to use them on any commoner who dared get too close to Pharaoh.

But this is no time to be scared, Mahu scolded himself. *Are you a man or still a boy? Where's your courage? Get in there and do what you came to do.*

Bracing his shoulders and lowering his head, he pushed his way through the crowd, getting closer to the vizier.

Closer to the heart scarab.

He could see its leather string around the old man's neck. Just one swipe of his knife, and it'd be his…

"Boy, get back. You're too close." Mahu felt a *medjay* place a hand roughly on his shoulder, pulling him back. The movement caught the attention of the vizier whose eyes widened in surprise. He recognised Mahu. One hand fluttered to his chest and grabbed the heart scarab through the fabric of his tunic. With the other hand, he summoned one of his personal guards.

"Take that ugly boy with the dirty tunic away. Make sure he doesn't come anywhere near me."

It's hopeless, thought Mahu as rough hands dragged him off his feet and he was dumped on the edge of the crowd. *I'll never get the amulet this far away from the vizier.*

His mind was in a whirl. Failure was no option. He had to do something to get the heart scarab. But what?

And then he had an idea, the sort he'd never had before.

General, he prayed. *If you want your amulet, help me. There's not much time left. I beg you, come to my aid. Quick!*

At first, nothing happened. The priests went on chanting, the crowd kept showering the holy statues with flowers.

Then a slight breeze ruffled Mahu's hair. A ghostly voice chuckled in his ear. "I am coming…"

The breeze got stronger, whipping sand off the ground. The priest's song faltered. The music stopped.

"There's a whirlwind coming, look," gasped

someone in the crowd.

Mahu looked up. The man in the crowd was right. There *was* a whirlwind coming. He could see a towering column of whirling sand and—for the briefest of moments—Mahu thought it looked like a mummy with torn, flapping bandages.

The crowd screamed and scattered as it found itself blinded by flying sand. Quickly, Mahu ripped the hem off his tunic and wrapped it around his face, leaving only a narrow slit for his eyes.

Then he plunged into the sea of panicked people. He ran unnoticed past the *medjay*, most of whom were trying to shield Pharaoh.

Astoundingly, the vizier was standing on his own, without his personal guard. Blinded by flying sand, he was struggling to keep the wig on his head. Mahu pulled his knife out from under his belt. In one deft move, he slashed the leather string from around his neck.

12

The Solar Barque
- Renni -

Renni squirmed along the tunnel in the general's tomb. This time he did not flinch as thick cobwebs brushed against his face and something crawled up his sidelock. He was prepared when the secret door opened in front of him. Landing on the sand, he got quickly to his feet. Mahu and Balaal tumbled to the ground after him.

Mahu whistled as he took in the riches around him. "You didn't tell me there was all this gold, little brother. It's enough to turn the holiest priest into a robber."

"Don't you dare touch anything," said Renni. "We've had enough trouble to last us a lifetime."

"But think what we could do with all this treasure," said Mahu. "We would be so happy."

Balaal looked from one boy to another. "It's true this man seems to have more gold than is fair. If my teachers are right, I understand he will use the chariot to ride around in his afterlife. He has gem-encrusted dishes to eat out of, richly decorated cups to drink from. Those mummified pets will come alive again to keep him entertained."

"Yes," said Renni. "And those gem-encrusted chests in the corner will be full of *shabti*. They will be his servants in the next world, to do his bidding and satisfy his every wish."

"A wealthy man indeed," said Balaal. "But you two are wealthier still. You have each other. From what you tell me, you have a mother who loves you very much. You, Renni, are skilled with the paintbrush. You, Mahu, have a love for the sea that will take you to the far corners of the world. Aren't those riches much more precious than all the treasures in this tomb?"

Renni thought about his work as a painter, about his uncle who would be worried and puzzled about his nephew missing a whole day's work. He hoped against hope Uncle Pepy would not fire him. "You are right," he said to Balaal. "Family and a purpose in life are the richest treasures in the world—and the next."

"I agree, little brother," said Mahu. "We might not be able to dine on duck or goose every day but we are rich in other ways." He pulled the heart scarab out of his tunic. "I think it might be midnight soon. Here. You know the exact spot where it was. You give it back to the general."

Renni picked his way to the sarcophagus which was still half-open. He reached inside and gently tucked the heart scarab safely between the bandages over the general's heart.

"Forgive me my crime, Your Honour," he said. "I hope I have returned it in time for the weighing of your heart against Ma'at's feather. I pray to the gods that you are allowed to continue your life in the world beyond."

A sigh echoed around the sarcophagus and Renni felt a rush of wind touch his face. The moonlight suddenly got brighter and the tassels on the umbrella moved.

"Look," said Balaal.

The distinct shape of a man rose from the coffin. It was dressed in a general's uniform with a helmet and a tiger-skin cloak. The heart scarab hung around its neck. It floated slowly, majestically, to the golden barque and stepped inside it. A ghostly dog took its place beside it, wagging its tail. A boatman appeared at the stern.

Somewhere above the children's heads a doorway opened, revealing a sky full of dazzling stars. The general looked up.

"If you meet our father in the afterlife," said Mahu, "please tell him that we love him and we miss him."

"Every day," added Renni.

A beam of moonlight shone down through

the doorway, filling the entire tomb with a light so bright, Renni had to shield his face with his hands. Peeping through his fingers, he saw a jackal-headed figure far away in the sky, waiting, the scales of justice dangling from one hand.

"Goodbye, general," Renni said, "and good luck."

The general touched the heart scarab at his chest and nodded a salute to the three children. Then the boatman started paddling and the solar barque carried him up into the sea of dazzling stars.

Epilogue

The vizier smashed his fist down on the table, sending glass bottles flying across the room. He hurled his curved wand to the floor. Curse the gods! They had failed him.

Hotep knocked on the door and entered the room hesitantly. "I've put the boy in the dungeon as you asked, master."

"Keep him there until I decide what to do with him," snapped the vizier. "Now leave me alone."

Hotep hurried out, picking his way through the shattered glass on the floor. The vizier marched up to the statue of Heka and spat in his offering bowl.

"For years I have honoured your name," he thundered. "I have offered you sacrifice. And what do I get in return? Disappointment! I was the one meant to be at Pharaoh's side, ruling the Black Land beside him. I was the one who should have shared his power and glory. Instead he chose his childhood friend. Tatia! The general.

"With his heart scarab, I would have destroyed his ka. I would have prevented him and Pharaoh ruling together in the afterlife. But you saw fit to thwart my plans. I was cheated of my revenge by those three stupid children.

"Children! I cannot believe the humiliation! But I shall win the day yet. I reject you, Heka, and I shall seek the help of a more powerful god."

Taking a lamp, the vizier opened a secret door in his study and hobbled down a dark flight of stairs until he reached a small room with no windows. It was completely empty save for a statue and a *stone altar in front of it.*

The vizier held up his lamp to gaze at the statue. The image of Set, the god of chaos and confusion glared back at him with dark obsidian eyes. The vizier bowed, placing both hands on the altar. "I pledge you my undying loyalty," he whispered. "I give you my life and my devotion. I reject all other gods except you."

The statue's polished eyes gleamed and slowly turned red. Set's sinister magic was working already.

"I was cheated of my revenge on General Tatia," the vizier whispered to the statue, "but my story is not finished yet. With your help, master of darkness, I shall yet rule the Black Land. And when I sit on Pharaoh's throne, I shall feed the kas of those three children to Ammut myself."

Renni, Mahu and Balaal's
adventures continue in

THE
CROCODILE
CURSE

GLOSSARY
& AUTHOR NOTES

Acacia • An expensive kind of wood.

Barque • A barque is a sailing ship usually with three masts. A solar barque is a much smaller boat which the Ancient Egyptians believed was used by the god Ra. He travelled in it across the sky. Pharaohs and powerful people placed barques in their tombs to carry them to the afterlife.

Beautiful Festival of the Valley • A festival honouring the dead. It was held every year in the city of Waset.

Black Land • The Ancient Egyptians called their country Kemet, which means the Black Land. The name was derived from the black silt that covered the fields after the floods. The deserts on either side of Egypt were called the Red Land.

Deben • A weight used during bartering at the market.

East Bank • The east side of the Nile where most of the Ancient Egyptians lived. As the sun rises in the East, it was considered the place of the living.

Faience • A type of pottery which was very popular in Ancient Egypt.

Fenkhu • A word that described an ancient people today known as Phoenicians. Their descendants are the people of Lebanon.

Hekau • Ancient magic, named after Heka, the god of magic. The word was also used to describe practitioners of magic, or magicians.

Hieroglyphs • A word of Greek origin that describes Ancient Egyptian writing. It means 'sacred carving'.

Ka • A part of the soul, or spirit, that survived a human being's death.

Kemet • See 'Black Land'.

Kush • The land of Kush lay south of Ancient Egypt. Its people were also called Kush. Today it's part of modern Egypt and Sudan.

Medjay • A policeman. Usually people from the land of Kush.

Mut • Mother.

Nesut–Towi • A vast temple complex dedicated to Amun-Ra and many other gods.

Royal Barge • A flat-bottomed boat used on rivers.

Sarcophagus • A stone coffin.

Sesh Qedut • An apprentice.

Sethi • Loincloth, a piece of material wrapped around the middle part of the body. A bit like a kilt.

Shabti • Little figurines representing a dead person's servants. They were buried with their masters in the hope that they would continue to serve in the afterlife.

Shaduf • A wooden structure used to draw water from the river.

Shenti • A fancy loincloth or kilt. Usually worn by the rich.

Sidelock • A lock of hair growing on one side of the head.

Sidelock Amulet • An amulet kept in a sidelock to protect and bring good luck.

Sphinx • A mythical creature with the body of a lion and the head of a human being.

Vizier • A high-ranking person who would rule and act on behalf of the pharaoh.

West Bank • The desert across the Nile from the main city of Waset was considered the land of dead. It was a vast cemetery.

ANCIENT EGYPTIAN GODS

The Ancient Egyptians believed in hundreds of gods and goddesses. Some were worshipped all over Ancient Egypt and some were honoured only in one region or city. Over time, the stories about the gods and their powers changed to suit the times. People believed they controlled their lives. Everyone, even Pharoah, was careful to show their respect, to please the gods and to live by their rules. Here is some information about the gods and goddesses mentioned in our story.

Ammut • Also called Ammit. She was a demon goddess who gobbled up the *ka* of dead people whose heart weighed heavier than Ma'at's feather. She had the chest of a lion, the body of a hippo, and her head was a crocodile's.

Amun-Ra • Amun-Ra was originally two gods: Amun, the god of air, and Ra (or Re), the sun god. After the Ancient Egyptians won a war against their neighbours, they thanked Amun by merging him with Ra, making him the most powerful god ever.

Anubis • The jackal-headed god who protected tombs and embalmers. He was the god of funerals and he held the scales of justice during a dead person's judgement.

Bast • Also called Bastet, she was the daughter of Ra and Isis. Originally a lion goddess, she eventually became a cat goddess. She had a whole city dedicated to her, called Bubastis.

Hathor • One of the most important goddesses of ancient Egypt, she was mother to Horus and Ra. Often depicted as a cow or with cow's horns on her head, she was also the goddess of joy, music and celebration. Most important of all, she was believed to protect mums-to-be and midwives.

Heka • Perhaps the most ancient of Ancient Egyptian gods, some believed he existed before time itself. He was the god of magic and magic rituals.

Isis • The goddess of magic, death and healing. One of the most beloved goddesses in Ancient Egypt, she was worshipped throughout the land. Also considered the mother of all pharaohs, she was often drawn with a small throne as her crown.

Khonsu • The moon god. His name means 'traveller' because he journeyed across the night sky.

Ma'at • Ma'at was the goddess of truth, wisdom and justice. Her symbols are a pair of scales and an ostrich feather. When a person died, their heart was weighed against Ma'at's feather to find out if they deserved to go into the afterlife.

Meretseger • The cobra-goddess. She protected the tombs on the West Bank of the Nile, especially the ones in the Valley of the Kings where the pharaohs were buried.

Mut • The mother goddess. The wife of Amun-Ra, her brothers and sisters included Bastet, Hathor and Ma'at. Khonsu and Montu were her sons. Some of her symbols are the cobra, the lioness and the double crown of Egypt.

Osiris • The god of many things. He protected the vegetation, the farms and farmers. He was also the god of the life, the afterlife and the dead. Pictures of him show him half-wrapped in mummy bandages and with green skin, to show he protected life on earth too.

Ra • The sun god. The Ancient Egyptians believed the sun was Ra sailing across the sky in his boat. At night, when the sun set, Ra travelled through the underworld and had to get past a snake-god called Apopis to rise again.

Set • Also known as Seth, was the god of the desert, storms, violence and disorder. He also protected all immigrants living and working in Ancient Egypt.

Sobek • The crocodile god. Often drawn as a powerful man with a crocodile's head, fishermen prayed to him so he would defend them against the dangers of the Nile. People offered him mummified crocodile eggs as gifts.

LOCATIONS AND CHARACTERS

The main characters in *The Heart Scarab* are figments of the author's imagination. Pharaoh Ramesses II was real, as was his grand vizier Paser. This story's vizier and his plots are fictional though. The real-life vizier Paser was indeed a hekau but no one knows if he used magic to obtain power. One of his shabtis is in the University College London collection.

The Artist's Village was close to the Valley of the Kings on the West Bank of the River Nile. Today its Arabic name is Deir el-Medina but most of the artists who lived in it called it simply Pa-Demi, 'the Village'. The Ancient Egyptians considered it a very special place. They believed the artists who lived in it were inspired by the gods to create beautiful art that honoured the pharaohs.

Crocodile Island is inspired by the many islands in the Nile. My favourite one is Philae, which had a beautiful temple dedicated to Isis. When the Aswan Dam was built, the temple was moved brick by brick to another island.

Amun-Ra's Temple was known to the ancient Egyptians as Nesut-Towi and Ipet-Isut. It is a vast complex of temples and other buildings. The main temples are dedicated to Amun-Ra, his wife Mut and their son Montu. Even today, visitors can still see the sacred lake, the avenue lined with stone sphinxes and a colossal statue of Ramesses the Great. The temple's name today is Karnak.

The Valley of the Kings is situated across the river from Waset, on the West Bank of the Nile. It was the burial ground for pharaohs, their families and other very important people. At least sixty two tombs have been discovered. They are all dug deep into the surrounding hills to protect their mummies and treasures from tomb robbers. The biggest known tomb in the valley was built to house the many children of Ramesses II. All the tombs were broken into over the years. The only one that survived intact was one of the smallest. It was the last resting place of a king called Tutankhamun. The riches found inside show us just how lavish a pharaoh's burial was.

Waset, now known as modern-day Luxor, was a very important city in Ancient Egypt for hundreds of years. Built on the East Bank of the Nile, it was one of the most important cities of the ancient world. Its palaces and temples were dazzling. Even in ruins, its temples remain famous to this very day.

LET'S PLAY SENET!

In Ancient Egypt, there weren't video games—they played a game called Senet! There are many variations of Senet but here's what you need if you want to play:

- A big piece of paper or cardboard
- Four lolly sticks
- Ten counters, five each of a colour

Only two people can play Senet.

The Board

Firstly, we have to make the board. Divide your piece of paper or card into a ten by three grid. Each box is called a 'house'. Next, draw special hieroglyphs in the squares shown on the next page. Each of these unique houses have special rules you have to follow.

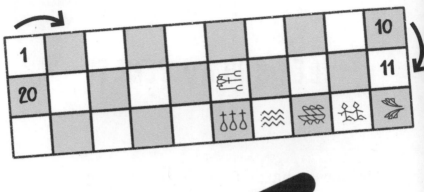

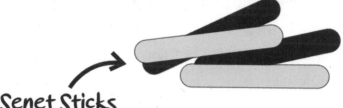

Senet Sticks

Take your four lolly sticks and paint or colour one side of each black. On the remaining sides, paint or colour them a bright colour.

The Rules

The first player to get all their counters off the board wins. To do this, move through the rows by starting at the top and going down to the next row when you reach the end. If you can move, you have to. Once you reach the last houses, you can attempt to remove your counter.

The number of squares you move is based on how you throw the senet sticks:

- Three black and one colour: 1 house, toss again.
- Two black and two colour: 2 houses
- Three colour and one black: 3 houses
- Four colour: 4 houses, toss again
- Four black: 5 houses, toss again

There are a few other rules to remember:

- Only one counter can be in a house at a time. You can move any of your counters during a turn.
- At the beginning of the game, you must place all the counters on the first row. They must alternate between player one and player two: for example, 1, 2, 1, 2, 1, 2, 1, 2, 1, 2.
- If you land on a house that already has a counter, you can capture it. The other player's counter is moved to where your counter was.
- You can only capture a house if there aren't two or more of the other player's counters next to one another. If there are, you cannot move.

The Hieroglyph Houses

There are six houses which have the following hieroglyphs. They have unique rules for when you land on them:

෮෮෮ The House of Happiness: each counter has to land on this house exactly or you cannot move forwards, and therefore cannot win.

≋ The House of Water: you have to move back to the House of Rebirth (⧈) and cannot move the counter until you choose to move it on another turn.

⧉ The House of Three Truths: throw your sticks again. If you have three colour sides up, you remove your counter from the board.

⚘ The House of Re-Atoum: throw your sticks again. If you have two colour sides up, you remove your counter from the board.

⟋ The Last House: throw your sticks again. You can only remove your counter when only one colour stick is facing up.

Have fun playing Senet!